Solomon Squirrel's
Amazing Chanukah Adventure

Jeffrey J. Lefko

Illustrations by Stephanie Burgess

This book is dedicated to my children and my grandchildren. They have inspired me to write a story about understanding others who are different from themselves. This story was written as much for parents as for their children.

Jeffrey J. Lefko

Solomon Squirrel got up early one particularly cold, snowy, winter morning. He had a lot to do. This was an exciting time for him and his family since he was preparing to surprise them. He tiptoed by Mommy Squirrel and the children squirrels. They were snuggled up on a big bed of leaves and branches. Today he had to hurry and scurry to collect enough nuts and acorns for his family. It had been very difficult to find enough nuts because the weather had turned colder earlier this year.

This morning he brought a bigger bag to collect special nuts and acorns to celebrate Chanukah- his children's favorite time of the year. They knew Solomon always tried to come up with fun surprises and something different for each of the eight nights of the celebration. This year he wanted so badly to find enough nuts and acorns to make their menorah, spinning dreidel tops, and other traditional Chanukah treats.

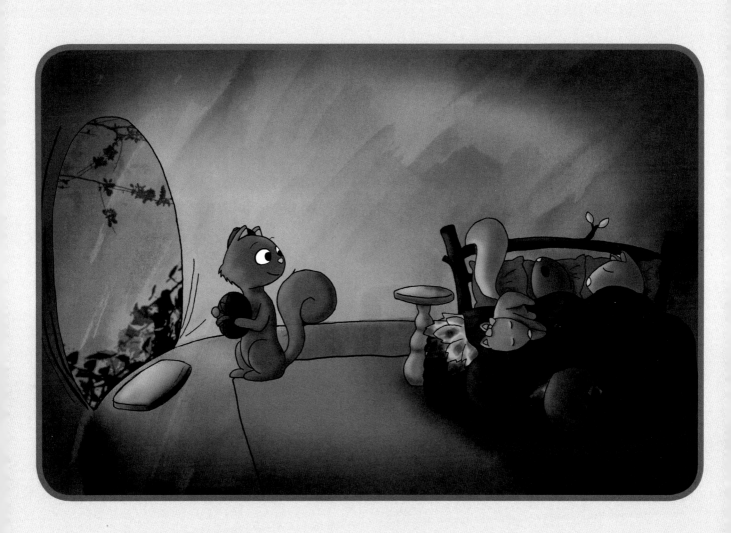

Solomon was convinced that this year's celebration was going to be the biggest and the best surprise for his family. He had been planning it since the leaves turned colors, the nights turned colder and the days grew shorter.

Solomon and his family lived in one of the tallest and biggest fir trees in the woods. It was a great place to live and he often thought, as he looked through the branches, that he could reach out and touch the stars and the moon since they shined ever so brightly and seemed so close to his home.

As he did every day, Solomon climbed down the gigantic tree passing several other squirrel families that lived in there too. Normally he did not stop to say anything to them because he was busy rushing off looking for nuts. However, this day he greeted the Stanley Squirrel family, the Steven Squirrel family and other squirrel families since he knew today was going to be special.

He could feel the excitement in the air and could tell by other squirrel fathers running around the woods looking for nuts and acorns too. Much to do and too little time to do it, he thought. He collected some nuts that he buried a few days ago and was on his way to find others he remembered from his daily trips. All the while, he imagined the smiles on his family's faces when they saw the special surprises.

Solomon spent the entire day looking for nuts and acorns, but he still hadn't filled his bag. He had to find more before he worked his way back.

He was busy searching for the special collection of nuts when he stopped in his tracks as he heard a strange, high-pitched noise throughout the forest.

"What was that noise?" He almost dropped the bag.

The sound grew louder and louder. Other squirrels heard it too and ran away bumping into each other. Solomon flung the bag around his back and hurried to his tree as quickly as his little legs could take him. Some of the nuts fell out of his bag. He didn't care. He had to get back to his family. He ran so fast; his little legs grew tired.

Everything seemed out of place as the high-pitched sound continued, but there was something else. He couldn't explain it... it sounded like... voices. Voices he'd heard before. Then he remembered. It was last year, during a trip to visit his relatives on the other side of the woods, when he heard the same kind of voices.

Finally, he reached his tree. He looked up, the tree seemed much taller than it normally did and his family seemed so far away. He started the long climb with his sack still on his back. He was losing more and more nuts with every step. He jumped from branch to branch, up and up, faster and further than ever before.

He ran inside to check on his family. They were huddled since they heard the same noises and were frightened. As soon as they saw him, they jumped up and ran to hug him.

"Daddy!" They all yelled together. They were a family again!

However, even though he was home, he could tell they didn't feel safe since the noises got louder, not so much the voices, but the high-pitched noise. No time for the Chanukah celebration now, Solomon thought. He tried to comfort them by suggesting that the noise was coming from the new squirrel neighbors who had teenage squirrels, and they made a lot of noise. That seemed to calm them down, particularly Mommy Squirrel.

Solomon still wondered what the noises were though. He grew increasingly worried when he felt the tree move and shake. Some of the leaves fell down like raindrops.

What could be causing that? Could it be those voices or the high-pitched noise? What was happening?

Just as Solomon had that thought, the tree fell. CRACKLE! CRASH! GA-BOOM! Then it stayed still.

Solomon ran over to his family who were upside down in their beds. The small ones giggled and thought it was fun to fall down and to get all jumbled up. "Let's do that again." They shouted.

But Solomon wasn't smiling. He was worried. What was going on?

The tree moved–again. This time it didn't fall, it was down on its side on—some type of big bed. This was the biggest and the loudest bed that Solomon had even seen or heard. It moved and kept moving and moving, farther and farther away. Where were they going and why were they leaving?

They moved for a long time and Solomon couldn't tell where they were. He was too frightened to look outside to catch a glimpse of the new world. After what seemed like a squirrel lifetime, the big bed came to a stop. Again, Solomon heard the voices; the tree moved again. This time, the bed moved up, higher up with the tree until it stopped with a SCREECH AND A SQUEAL! The little ones shouted. "Let's do THAT again". Solomon told them to be quiet and listened carefully for the next sounds.

All was silent.

Nighttime approached, and their eyes became heavier and heavier. The entire Solomon Squirrel family fell fast asleep. After what they had been through, they slept for a long time.

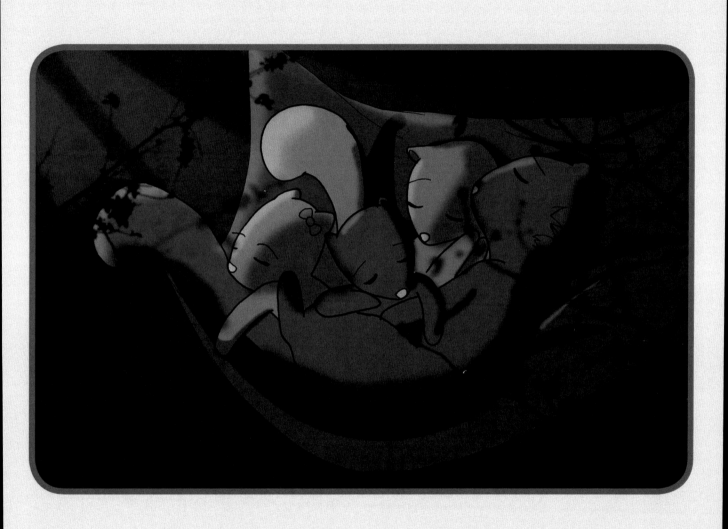

Solomon awoke when he heard new voices and noises. They were different, beautiful and magical. He heard music and songs. He rubbed his eyes as he saw rays of light, different colors were streaming through his home and onto the beds. There were blue, white, green, red, and yellow lights. He saw sights and heard sounds like none he had even seen or heard. The little ones thought it was the special celebration he put together for Chanukah; Solomon knew different though he still didn't know what was going on.

He finally got enough courage and went to the end of the house. He peered through the branches to see outside. He opened them wider to see as much of the outside as possible. Different kinds of people surrounded the tree. They were different sizes too. They held hands, sung songs, smiled, laughed, clapped, and hugged each other, just like his family does.

You see, Solomon's Most Amazing Adventure was really about Solomon's Most Amazing Discovery. What Solomon Squirrel didn't know then, but soon discovered from those new voices, was that their beautiful tree, his home, was picked as the National Christmas Tree to be moved and replanted on the grounds of the White House in Washington, DC, where the President of the United States and his family lives. Every year, his majestic tree would be decorated for the holidays.

He saw that the other squirrel families made the same adventurous trip, and they too were peering through branches. He realized that the other squirrel families were celebrating in their own way. Steven Squirrel's family was celebrating Christmas and the Stanley Squirrel family was celebrating Kwanza. Other squirrel families celebrated in other ways too.

It was finally time for Solomon's family to have their own special celebration of Chanukah. They prayed with their menorah and played with their dreidels all night long. They hugged and kissed each other. They were safe, they were together, and they felt happy in their new home.

Solomon and his family also liked their new "woods" so much. Happily, they were all joined by other squirrel families who wanted to live in this special tree too. There were plenty of nuts and acorns to go around now, more than enough to share with all of the other squirrel families.

Most importantly, what Solomon discovered through his Most Amazing Chanukah Adventure, was that all of the squirrel families celebrated their holidays differently. Many of them were praying in their own special ways for the same things, Peace on Earth and Good Will for all creatures, big and small.

Solomon, his family and the other squirrel families in that wonderful tree were truly blessed this holiday season and every season after. They discovered each other, and how similar they were and all that they share together as one.

As Solomon and his family settled in for a long, restful slumber, they heard the beautiful songs and prayers of the holidays coming from both inside and outside their beautiful tree.

He turned to his family and at long last said, "Happy Chanukah".

What Solomon Squirrel discovered in his Most Amazing Chanukah Adventure are the most amazing gifts of every holiday season.

Author:

Jeffrey J. Lefko

He has been fine tuning his skills at juggling multiple "balls in the air" over the last twenty years since he wrote *Solomon Squirrel's Amazing Chanukah Adventure*. He was determined to publish his book without eventually dropping the ball. Besides, his arms were getting very tired.

Illustrator:

Stephanie Burgess

She is a Kindergarten Teacher's Aide in Maryland. When she is not mending the broken hearts of 5 year olds, she is either drawing, taking pictures, or making movies.

Made in the USA
Columbia, SC
23 November 2022

71385240R00018